W9-AGU-656

The Great Valentine Mystery

Written by Megan E. Bryant

Illustrated by Mindy M. Pierce

Grosset & Dunlap · New York

ISBN 0-448-43281-1   A B C D E F G H I J

It's Valentine's Day! All of the kids in Ms. Jacobs's class are so excited—they can't wait for their special Valentine's party.

"We still have a lot to do before the party," Ms. Jacobs tells the class.

"First, let's decorate the classroom!"

"I brought balloons!" says Beth.

"I brought streamers!" Angela says.

"And I brought pretty flowers!" says Susan.

"Flowers? *Eww!*" says Carl.

"The classroom looks great," Ms. Jacobs says with a smile.
"Is it time for the party?" Robby asks.

"Not yet. We'll have the party after lunch," Ms. Jacobs tells everyone.
"But it *is* time to deliver your valentines!"
"Valentines? *Eww!*" says Pete.

The art teacher has a special activity today.
"We're all going to do an art project together!" he explains.
"We'll make a big Valentine's mural. You can hang it up in
your classroom for the party."

"I'm going to draw school," Jordan says.
"I'm going to draw Cupid!" Marie says.
"Cupid? *Eww!*" says Mike.

It's time for gym!
"Everybody, make two teams," calls the coach. "We're going to play Valentine's Soccer. One team is the Hugs, and the other team is the Kisses!"

"Valentine's Soccer-awesome!" cheers Stephanie.
"Hugs? Kisses? *Eww!*" Matt says.

In music class, there is more Valentine's fun.
The kids sing "I Love You, a Bushel and a Peck" and
"Love Makes the World Go Round."
"Love? *Eww!*" says Sam.

On the way to lunch, Ms. Jacobs takes the class by the nurse's office.

"Happy Valentine's Day, kids!" the nurse says.
"Line up so I can listen to your hearts."
"Hearts? *Eww!*" Paul says.

At lunch, everyone keeps talking about the party.

No one eats dessert because there will be
lots of cookies and cupcakes later. Yum!

After lunch, the kids play outside.
Brrr! It's cold today!
Then—at last!—it's time for the party!

Everyone hurries back to the classroom.
Wait! Something's wrong!

"Look! The treats are missing!" shouts Carl.
Ms. Jacobs smiles at the class. "Don't worry," she says.
"I know where they are!"

Ms. Jacobs takes the class to the cafeteria.

"Now we can all decorate the treats," she says. "Happy Valentine's Day!"
"Treats? Yay!" yell all the kids.

Once everyone is back in the classroom, the party can finally start.
But wait! Something else is missing—Piggie the hamster!
"Oh, no!" exclaims Ms. Jacobs.
"I must have left the cage door open after I fed her!"

"Don't worry," Dan shouts. "I see where she is!"
Ms. Jacobs laughs when she sees the hamster in the mailbox.
"I guess Piggie wanted to come to the party, too!"

There are lots of fun things to do with pom-pom stickers! Follow the instructions to make your very own Valentine's crafts. Make sure to cover the space where you work with old newspapers and always wear a smock to protect your clothing. Remember to ask an adult for permission before starting any of these projects. Have fun!

Valentine Heart Pencil Toppers

What you'll need:
Red, white, or pink construction paper

Scissors   Glue   Pencils

Pom-pom stickers

What to do:
1. Fold a piece of construction paper in half.

2. Cut out a heart that is 2½ inches across (since the paper is folded in half, you will have two identical hearts).

3. Glue the two hearts together, but leave the pointed end open (that's the part you'll place on the pencil). At the point, you should have a ¼-inch hole.

4. When the glue is dry, pop the pencil topper onto your favorite pencil and decorate it with sparkly pom-pom stickers!

Valentine Bookmark

What you'll need:
Colored cardboard

Scissors   Glue

Construction paper or magazine cutouts

Pom-pom stickers

What to do:
1. Have an adult help you cut out a cardboard rectangle that is 2 inches wide and 7 inches long.

2. Glue the cutouts to the bookmark.

3. Stick two or three pom-pom stickers on the top edge of the bookmark.

Valentine Picture Frame

What you'll need:
A 7- by 9-inch piece of cardboard

Scissors   Glue   Tape

Construction paper, tissue paper, or wrapping paper cutouts

Pom-pom stickers

What to do:
1. Have an adult help you cut out a 5- by 7-inch hole from the center of the cardboard.

2. Glue the cutouts to the cardboard frame. Make sure you cover all the cardboard!

3. Tape your favorite photo to the inside of the frame.

4. Decorate the finished frame with pom-pom stickers.